Berry's Halloween Costume Trouble
Read-Along
STORYBOOK AND CD

This is the story of a bunny named Berry. You can read along with me in your book. You will know it's time to turn the page when you hear this sound. . . . Let's begin now.

Editorial by Eric Geron   Design by Lindsay Broderick

Copyright © 2016 Disney Enterprises, Inc. All rights reserved. Published by Disney Press, an imprint of Disney Book Group.
No part of this book may be reproduced or transmitted in any form or by any means, electronic or mechanical, including photocopying, recording, or by any information storage and retrieval system, without written permission from the publisher.
For information address Disney Press, 1101 Flower Street, Glendale, California 91201.
Printed in the United States of America
First Paperback Edition, July 2016   10 9 8 7 6 5 4 3 2 1
Library of Congress Control Number: 2015960530
ISBN 978-1-4847-4707-0   FAC-008598-16162

For more Disney Press fun, visit www.disneybooks.com
Download the Whisker Haven Tales App

Disney PRESS

Los Angeles · New York

SUSTAINABLE
FORESTRY
INITIATIVE

Certified Chain of Custody
At Least 20% Certified Forest Content
www.sfiprogram.org
SFI-00993
For Text Only

One fine evening in Whisker Haven, all the Palace Pets and Critterzens were abuzz. For it was Hallow Haven, a night of spooky delights and spectacular costumes.

The Pawlace was decorated with cobwebs and jack-o'-lanterns, and the friends couldn't wait to celebrate!

Berry the bunny entered the Throne Room. "I can't wait to start baking the Hallow Haven cake!"

Then Berry bumped into Slipper. The cat was dressed in a bedazzled gown. "Happy Hallow Haven, Slipper! Your costume is simply dazzling!"

Next Berry turned to see Daisy dressed
as an artist with a beret and a smock. "Ooh!
Your costume is very artistic, Daisy!"

Matey walked over dressed as a dashing sea captain, and Berry
grinned. "And your costume is *sea*-sational, Matey!"

Berry's friends looked at her and smiled. "Thanks, Berry!"

Just then, Ms. Featherbon flew into the Throne Room dressed as a witch.

"Happy Hallow Haven, Berry!"

Berry hopped with joy at the sight of her. "Happy Hallow Haven, Ms. Featherbon! Your costume is wickedly wonderful!"

"Thank you! Every pet is making such splendificent costumes for the Hallow Haven Costume Show!"

Ms. Featherbon looked Berry up and down.

"Oh! But Berry! Where is *your* costume?"

"Nuts and berries! I was so busy thinking about baking the Hallow Haven cake that I forgot about my costume!"

Slipper stepped closer to Berry. "It's okay, Berry. We'll help you come up with something brilliant!"

Matey chimed in next. "But the show is starting soon, so we better hurry!"

The friends quickly got to work.

First Slipper helped Berry try on a costume that was not quite Berry's flavor.

Next it was Daisy's turn to help! She whipped up another costume for Berry to wear. Berry looked down at it and shook her head.

Lastly, Matey helped Berry try on something *sea*-sational!
"What *am* I, Matey?"
"A mer-bunny, of course!"

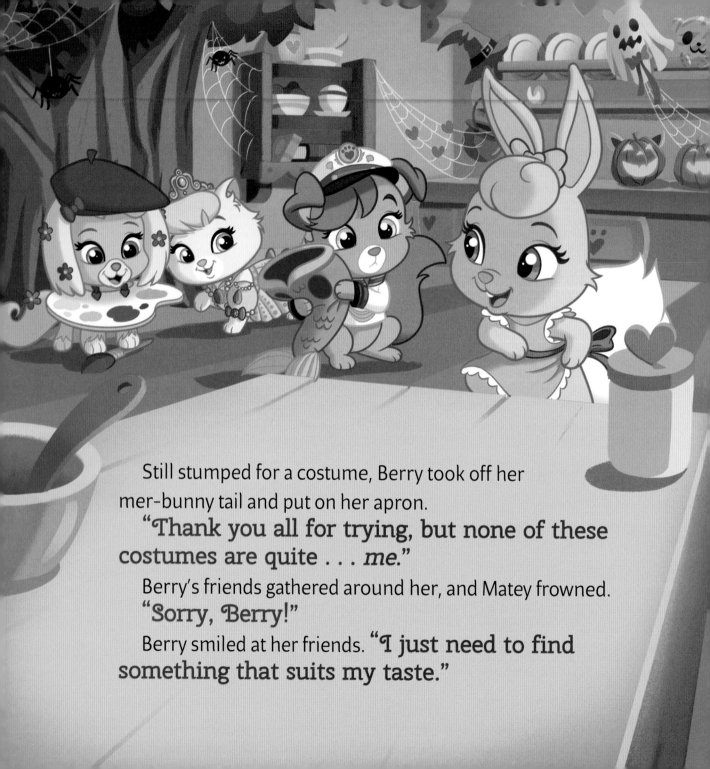

Still stumped for a costume, Berry took off her mer-bunny tail and put on her apron.

"Thank you all for trying, but none of these costumes are quite . . . *me*."

Berry's friends gathered around her, and Matey frowned. "Sorry, Berry!"

Berry smiled at her friends. "I just need to find something that suits my taste."

Suddenly, Berry had a thought.

"Taste! Butter beans! I've still got to bake the Hallow Haven cake!"

Daisy knew what to do! "We can help you, Berry!"

She got out eggs as Berry got out a bowl.

Matey grabbed the flour and sugar.

And Slipper found the berries.

As the friends gathered the ingredients and began mixing them, Berry smiled with joy! She stirred everything together, then poured the batter into pans and put them in the oven.

Soon the batter bubbled up and turned a beautiful golden brown. Berry let the cake cool and then got to work frosting and decorating it. As she did so, she started to worry.

"Well, we finished the Hallow Haven cake, but I still don't have a costume for the costume show. I certainly can't go covered in frosting!"

Matey, Daisy, and Slipper looked at each other, then at the messy kitchen, and smiled.

"Yes, you can!"

Berry looked at her friends, stunned. "What do you mean?"

Slipper smiled even wider and glanced at the others. "We know just what your costume should be! C'mon!"

Berry, Matey, Slipper, and Daisy put their paws in together.

"Hearts! Hooves! Paws!"

The first stop on the list was visiting **Tillie's Tutu Tailor** in Whisker Haven Village.

There Slipper, Matey, and Daisy told **Tillie** all about Berry's costume conundrum.

Tillie knew just what to do. She snipped some fabric and ribbons . . .

and sewed some pieces together until. . .

. . . ta-da!
Berry had her berry own costume!

Back at the Pawlace, it was time for the **Hallow Haven Costume Show**. All the Palace Pets and Critterzens gathered around the runway in their *spook*-tacular costumes. They were eagerly waiting for the show to begin when Ms. Featherbon flew into the hall, took out a horn, and blew into it. *Oooooo!*

"Happy Hallow Haven! The festivities will begin
with our annual Hallow Haven Costume Show!"

The Palace Pets and Critterzens cheered!

With one last honk of her horn, Ms. Featherbon signaled for the show to begin!

On the runway, Petite strutted out dressed as **a ghost**.

Sultan came next dressed as **a dinosaur**.

Dreamy followed wearing her favorite accessory—**a pillow**!

Then Treasure came bounding out dressed as **a vampire bat**.

And Pumpkin was all dolled up in **a glamorous ball gown**!

It was a costume show unlike any other.

Finally, it was Berry's turn to walk the runway in her costume. She was dressed in her baker's best as a **confection**—with **a cake on her head**!

Ms. Featherbon admired Berry's good taste. *"Oooh!"*

Then Slipper, Matey, and Daisy hit the runway in their original costumes, now with royally wonderful **confection costume hats**!

Ms. Featherbon couldn't contain her excitement at the sight of them all.

"Splendificent!"

The confection costume crew did another strut down the runway, and **everyone applauded**.

Ms. Featherbon flew up to the group. "Where did you all get the idea for those confection concoctions?"

Matey, Daisy, and Slipper all pointed to Berry.

"Berry's baking!"

Berry smiled.

"But I would have never come up with it
without the help of my friends."

Ms. Featherbon flew around the cake hats, licking her beak.

"They look good enough to eat!"

Berry quickly wheeled out her Hallow Haven cake.

"You can't eat them, Ms. Featherbon, but you sure can eat the Hallow Haven cake!"

Everyone cheered as they headed over for some cake.

"Happy Hallow Haven!"